for Grandpa Terry

Calling all artists
enjoy the space.

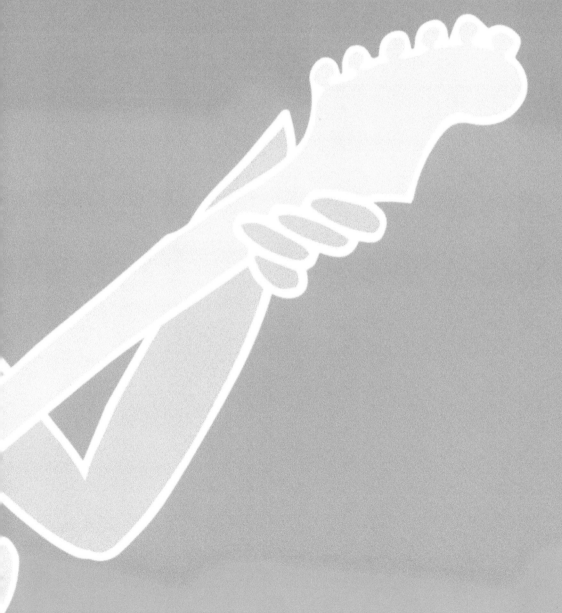

This is an
open canvas place.

As for your twinkle
shimmer sparkle

your light
your warmth
appreciates.

All you composers
bring your composure.

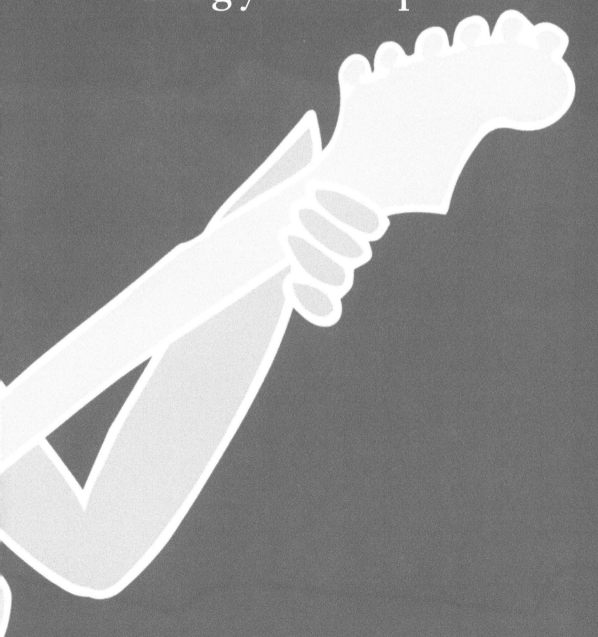

# This is a story
## well underway.

As for your
brushstrokes

splashes
auroras

you are invited
to co-create.

I am.

I am on my way.

I am.

I am on my way.

# Calling all consciousness bring your finesse.

This is a graceful
grateful place.

# This is a blast
## this bliss
## this blessing.

This is a sacred
naked space.

This is a pleasant
present place

made for the swan
skywalker starchild

made for the sufi
singer seer

made for the wild
colors flying.

I am.

I am on my way.

CPSIA information can be obtained
at www.ICGtesting.com
Printed in the USA
BVHW021001260820
587379BV00023B/410

9 781087 905334